JAN   2008

This book belongs to:

_____

Digital art by Callaway Animation Studios under the direction of David Kirk
in collaboration with Nelvana Limited.

This book is based on the TV episode "Bedtime Story," written by Scott Kraft, from the animated TV series *Miss
Spider's Sunny Patch Friends* on Nick Jr., a Nelvana Limited/Absolute Pictures Limited co-production in association
with Callaway Arts & Entertainment, based on the Miss Spider books by David Kirk.

Nicholas Callaway, President and Publisher
Cathy Ferrara, Managing Editor and Production Director
Toshiya Masuda, Art Director • Nelson Gomez, Director of Digital Services
Joya Rajadhyaksha, Associate Editor • Amy Cloud, Associate Editor
Bill Burg, Digital Artist • Keith McMenamy, Digital Artist • Christina Pagano, Digital Artist
Raphael Shea, Senior Designer • Krupa Jhaveri, Designer

Special thanks to the Nelvana staff, including Doug Murphy, Scott Dyer, Tracy Ewing, Pam Lehn,
Tonya Lindo, Mark Picard, Jane Sobol, Luis Lopez, Eric Pentz, and Georgina Robinson.

Library of Congress Cataloging-in-Publication Data available upon request.

Distributed in the United States by Viking Children's Books.

Callaway Arts & Entertainment, its Callaway logotype,
and Callaway & Kirk Company LLC are trademarks.

ISBN 0-448-44367-8

Visit Callaway Arts & Entertainment at www.callaway.com

10 9 8 7 6 5 4 3 2 1   06 07 08 09 10

First edition, August 2006

Printed in China by ORO editions

Bedtime Story

David Kirk

CALLAWAY

NEW YORK

2006

It was bedtime, but the Cozy Hole was still abuzz!

"We have to speed up this routine," Holley sighed.

Miss Spider agreed. "Maybe a wishing web would help!"

iss Spider and Holley created a giant web. It was divided into eight sections, with one flower for each bug.

"If you go to bed on time, your flower moves up the web," Holley explained.

"Once it gets to the top, you can go to the Compost Day Fair!" Miss Spider smiled.

The children cheered.

That night, Miss Spider's buggies went to bed right on time. Soon they were sleeping as snug as bugs in rugs!

"Now it's our turn to go to bed," Miss Spider whispered to Holley. "But first I need to bake tea cakes."

"And I need to tidy up the Cozy Hole," Holley sighed.

"Oh my!" Miss Spider yawned as she took her tea cakes out of the oven. "What time is it?"

"Way past our bedtime!" said Holley as they crawled upstairs.

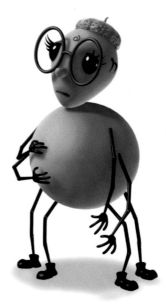

The next morning, Shimmer, Squirt, and Pansy woke early and started making breakfast.

"Where are Mom and Dad?" Shimmer wondered.

"Oh no," yawned Miss Spider as her buggy bunch tiptoed in. "We must have stayed up too late."

"Maybe you need a wishing web, too!" said Bounce.

That evening, Miss Spider and Holley got their very own wishing web.

"We're going to help you get to the top," said Squirt proudly.

"And your reward will be a morning to sleep in," said Bounce.

Miss Spider and Holley liked the sound of that!

When Miss Spider called her children to bed, she was surprised to see all eight of them lined up and ready.

"Are you and Dad ready for sleepy time, too?" asked Bounce.

"Well, I have some tea party invitations to make," Miss Spider admitted.

"We'll help!" said Squirt.

"Snuggle-bug time!" Bounce announced when the invitations were done.

"Uh-oh," mumbled Holley. "I promised Mr. Mantis that I would collect seeds for his class tomorrow."

"We can help with that, too," Squirt assured him.

They crawled to the moonlit meadow.

Dragon found fuzzy dandelion seeds, and Squirt gathered grass seeds. Shimmer brought a leaf full of orchid seeds—the smallest seeds in the world.

"Perfect!" said Holley.

"Time to sleep!" Squirt ordered when they returned to the Cozy Hole.

"I want a bedtime story!" said Holley.

Bounce started telling the tale of Goldigrub and the Three Gnats. Before he could finish, everybuggy was fast asleep.

Miss Spider and Holley woke the next morning to the sound of a tulip trumpet.

"Up and at 'em, out of bed, and soon you'll be at the top of the web!" Dragon shouted.

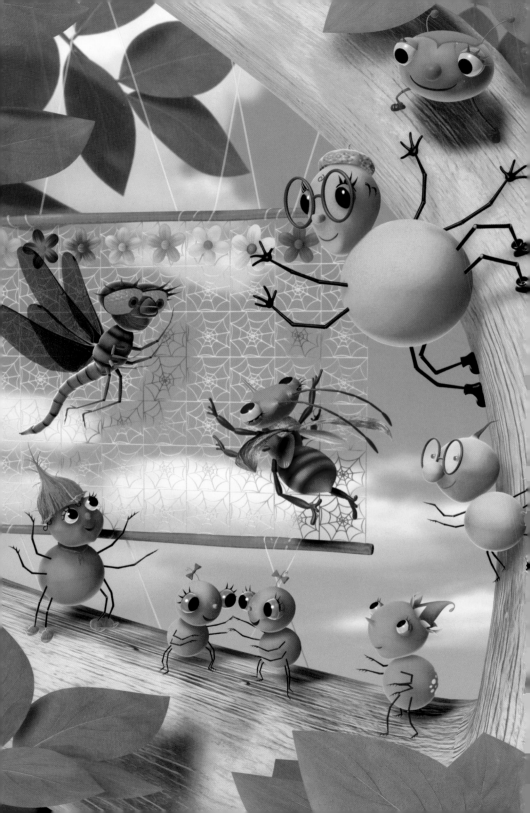

Over the next week, the Spider children went to bed on time, and made sure their parents did, too. Slowly, their flowers moved up the web, until finally . . .

"You all reached the top!" announced Holley.

"Compost Day Fair, here we come!" everybuggy cheered.

"Only one more night until
you're at the top, Mom and Dad,"
Shimmer said.

"But we can't miss the firefly
ballet tonight!" said Miss Spider.

The children looked at her sternly.

"Okay, we'll go another time,"
she said with a smile.

The next morning, Grandma Betty came over to take the little bugs to the fair. They all tiptoed out the door.

Miss Spider and Holley—who had reached the top of the wishing web—were snoring soundly upstairs.